A Trip to the Hot Springs

A MARSHMALLOW THE MAGICAL CAT ADVENTURE

By Kimberly Brayman

Illustrated by Irina Denissova

For information regarding permission please email Dr. Kimberly Brayman: info@ KimberlyBraymanAuthor.com

For bulk and wholesale orders please email Dr. Kimberly Brayman: info@KimberlyBraymanAuthor.com

ISBN: 978-1-951688-20-2

Written by: Dr. Kimberly Brayman
Illustrated by: Irina Denissova

Disclaimer: This book is not intended to replace a medical doctor, psychologist or therapist. Lovely, anxious, perfect-as-they-are children may benefit from seeing a counselor in person to learn strategies specific to their struggles. This book is intended only as a story to help normalize the struggle of living with anxiety. This book mentions some interventions such as belly breathing, desensitization (which should only be done with a professional), relaxation in a hot spring, having a growth mindset, and how the support of good friends can help.

Paperback team published with
Artistic Warrior Publishing
artisticwarrior.com

Dedicated to the dozens of lovely, sensitive, introverted
girls I have worked with over the years.
Anxiety, like an unwanted guest, often sat in the room
while we talked, even while skills and strategies grew.

Table of Contents

Chapter 1: Planning a Trip

"All true adventures start with a challenge," Marshmallow said to Avry. Penelope, the fairy, hovered nearby, wanting to help.

Avry sighed. "But I'm struggling, Marshmallow. I'm getting more and more anxious this spring. The kids at school are teasing me. I'm becoming afraid of new things: tall buildings, dark places, and tunnels."

Although Marshmallow appeared to be half asleep, he was listening. Avry's breathing was shallow and quick, and from this Marshmallow knew she was anxious. She sighed again and said, "It feels very, *very* hard."

Marshmallow purred from deep in his chest and crawled onto Avry's lap. "The weight of my warm, cuddly, magnificent self will relax her," he said to Penelope. "And that is true. I'm not boasting."

"Oh, Marshmallow. It's true you are magnificent," Penelope said. She hoped Marshmallow would let her ride on his back later.

"Hmmm," Marshmallow said. "What to do, what to do?" He turned to Avry and spoke to her in his magical way. "You chew your nails in the day and toss and turn at night, Avry."

Avry shrugged. She gently moved Marshmallow from her lap to the bed. She felt helpless, but it was time to go to school.

She picked up her backpack and, dragging her feet, headed down the stairs and out the door to the school bus.

"This is a challenge," Marshmallow said to Penelope. "We need to help."

Marshmallow picked up a pen in his mouth and went over to the house phone. He was glad Avry liked old things and had an old land-line telephone in her room. He slowly pushed the numbers Avry had scribbled by the phone. It rang two times. "Hello?" said a voice. It sounded like Nana.

"Nana," he meowed into the phone. "Are you there? We need help."

Nana listened closely. "Yes, Marshmallow, I hear you. I'll make the arrangements. You can both come to visit me over spring break. We'll go to the hot springs. Everyone relaxes at the hot springs."

"Thank you," Marshmallow meowed. "We knew you would help." He hung up the phone. "Penelope, we should pack for our marvelous trip while Avry is at school."

Marshmallow dragged a suitcase and a backpack out of the closet. He dropped in swim towels and suntan lotion. He gathered up Avry's shorts, T-shirts and hats. He packed her crocs for walking beside the pool, and warm sweaters for afterwards. "Where, oh where, are our sunglasses?"

"Lost?" offered the kind fairy. Avry and Marshmallow tended to leave things in different places. "Or maybe the elves took them."

Nana called Avry's mom and dad and asked if Avry could come for a visit. Then Nana called Atreus's mom and dad and asked if he could come too.

A Trip to the Hot Springs: A Marshmallow the Magic Cat Adventure

Once she was done, Nana flew into a flurry of activity. She was so excited her grandchildren were coming to visit. She went to the grocery store and bought their favorite snacks for the car ride. She asked the neighbor if he would watch her house. She talked to the fairies and trolls and unicorns.

Nana made a coffee and sat down. "What else will we need?" she asked the fairies that were sitting and having tea at her kitchen table.

"We will have more banana bread, if you please," the roundest fairy said.

The skinniest fairy let out a gentle burp as she slurped on her tea.

Nana sighed. The fairies were not helping. She left them to their tea.

"Hot springs . . . hmmmm. We will all need sunglasses."

Nana went into her cupboard of magical things. She pulled out four pair of sunglasses. There was a pink pair for Avry, a blue pair for Atreus, purple for Marshmallow, and orange for her. She took some scissors out of the drawer and cut off the *magical things* tags.

A Trip to the Hot Springs: A Marshmallow the Magic Cat Adventure

Chapter 2: Avry's Anxiety

At lunchtime, Avry sat at the side of the school playground, near the fence. She tucked her legs underneath her. She softened her belly. A the little squirrel crept over to sit beside her. "Oh, hello there," Avry said, as she focused on taking long, slow breaths.

The squirrel tickled Avry's hand with his little wet nose and sat closer.

"Thank you," Avry said. "Being tickled by your licks helps."

The squirrel looked up at her, as though it was listening.

"I have anxiety. I get overstimulated sometimes. I feel shaky. I often want to hide or run away. Sometimes I can't breathe because my heart is pounding so loud. I know when my hands get numb and when I can't find the right words, I'm anxious."

The little squirrel nodded. "Yup, that's true," he said.

"I feel so many things," Avry said, "and the kids here are too loud."

The squirrel nodded again.

Avry slowed her breathing and started to notice the warmth of the sun on her shoulders.

"What do you see and smell and hear?" asked the squirrel.

"I see bright green grass," Avry said. "I smell hot bread from the bakery next door. I hear the birds singing. I feel the prickly grass. It helps when we play this game," she said, smiling. Then the bell rang and Avry groaned. It was time to go back into the school.

Avry managed to get through her afternoon. At reading time, she went to a far-away land and met a prince. She could feel the small crown on top of her head, and she imagined stepping on to the magic carpet to go for a ride.

Before she knew it, the afternoon bell rang. The kids broke out in loud conversation. Avry darted to grab her backpack and rushed out the door.

Chapter 3: A Little Embarrassed, A Little Happy

"Avry, today is the day you see Dr. Kimberly again," Mama said in the car.

Avry felt a little embarrassed, a little happy, and a lot relieved. She added her therapist to her list of friends, or kind-of friends. "Dr. Kimberly always listens to me, Mama."

Her mama smiled warmly.

"She always tells me the truth, and she never ever tells me that what I'm feeling is not okay."

"Dr. Kimberly gave me a list of things to help you Avry." Her mama pulled out the list. "I'm never to say 'get over it,' or 'there is nothing to worry about,' or 'you are a big girl, you can handle it.'"

"Those things don't help, Mama."

"I know Avry, but sometimes it's hard to know what to say to help you. I love you so much."

Avry and her mama pulled up to the little blue building. Avry ran up the ramp and in the front door and into Dr. Kimberly's office. She pulled up a chair to the puzzle table and her mama made her hot chocolate.

Marshmallow walked in and sat beside her. "I will help you," he said, and his eyes went up and down in two different directions.

"I got two puzzle pieces in, Dr. Kimberly," Avry said.

"You are a smart girl," Dr. Kimberly said, smiling. "Anything to tell me?" she asked Avry's mom.

"Yes," Mama said. "Avry is going to go stay with her nana for a few days. I was hoping you could talk about it today."

"Oh, Mama," Avry said. "I love visiting Nana."

A dreamy look came over Avry's face as she thought of Nana's magic cupboard. There were paints and stencils. There was clay and crayons. There was white paper and colored paper. There were crafts and hula hoops. It would be fun.

Chapter 4: Oh No! Tunnels!

"When Avry and her cousin Atreus get to their nana's place, they are going to go visit the hot springs," Mama told Dr. Kimberly.

Avry thought of all the tunnels they had to go through to go the hot springs. "Oh no, Mama. Tunnels!"

Avry knew that avoiding all the things she was scared of was impossible, but she felt nervous.

Avry walked over to Dr. Kimberly and said, "I have strategies." Dr. Kimberly had taught her that word.

"I talk to my best friend, Stefan," Avry said. "I talk to my cousin, Atreus. Marshmallow helps me breathe in my belly. Mama and Daddy help by hugging me and talking to me. But I can't talk to the other kids at school about what I'm afraid of. They'll make fun of me."

"How do the things you mentioned help you?" Dr. Kimberly asked.

"Atreus is older," Avry said. "He helps me with my thinking. He says we can change my silly thoughts. I told him I didn't think I'd ever feel better. Then Atreus and I played a game, and I felt better. He reminded me that no one has anxiety all the time. He was right. Sometimes, it feels like I do have anxiety all the time."

Dr. Kimberly nodded.

"Marshmallow and Stefan go to the lake with me. If I'm super upset, I sit by the lake or walk in the woods and I feel better."

"Grounding into the earth helps," Dr. Kimberly agreed.

Avry thought grounding was a silly word but she tucked it away to think about later.

"What else can you do to help yourself?" asked Dr. Kimberly.

Avry thought. "If I wear sunglasses when it's really bright, it helps. If I wear earplugs if it's super loud, it helps. If Mama and

Daddy sit at the edge of the restaurant and not the middle, it helps. Staying out of big crowds helps, too."

"You have many good strategies, Avry. You need to use them, and ask for help when you need it," Dr. Kimberly said.

"I'm making a list of strategies for our trip," Marshmallow said with a pen in his mouth. He was writing all these things down, and feeling important. "Together, we can handle this."

Avry felt better as she joined her mama who was working on the puzzle.

"Ready?" Mama asked.

"Yes," Avry said.

Chapter 5: Nana's House

Penelope the fairy stayed home as she didn't like to travel. Avry and Marshmallow hugged her goodbye and then Avry was on her way to Nana's. When she arrived, the first person she saw was her cousin, Atreus. He had arrived just before her.

Marshmallow purred as they walked up the path to the front porch. Atreus ran to greet them, laughing. "Hello, hello," he said. "We're going to the hot springs!"

Avry smiled. She had packed some special things: cat treats for Marshmallow; a frisbee for Atreus, and a blow-up raft for Nana so she could float in the hot springs.

Nana was dressed in her funky pants and big dangly earrings. Her overnight bag was beside her. A big mug of coffee in her hand, a smile on her face, she laughed and did a happy dance, spilling her coffee. "We are going to the hot springs," she sang. "We are going on an adventure."

Nana handed them all the brand-new magical sunglasses.

Avry put on her sunglasses, looked outside and giggled. "There are two unicorns eating the grass on your lawn, Nana."

"I never did like mowing," Nana said.

Atreus put his sunglasses on. "There are two little garden trolls sitting on the top of the metal bull in your garden, Nana."

"I never did like weeding my garden," Nana said. "You need to get back to work," she said to the garden trolls.

Marshmallow put his sunglasses on and purred louder. "Oh,

I can see better," he said. He always saw fairies around him like little flicks of light, but now the magic things were really clear. There was a whole line of fairies flying off together, and three baby dragons sitting having tea on the edge of the garden wall.

The children sighed with contentment.

"Nana, your house is full of magic," Atreus said.

"The whole world is full of magic," Nana said. The magic sunglasses just help you see what is already there. Now grab your things and hop in the car."

Chapter 6: A Soccer Game

"Off we go," Nana said. The four of them drove through the streets of the town towards the mountains. Neighbors smiled and waved. Garden trolls were weeding gardens and unicorns were everywhere, eating the grass on front lawns.

"What a great town to visit," Avry said.

Nana drove slowly. She was looking for the smoothie shop.

She found it and soon everyone was back in the car with their

favorite smoothie. "These are full of fruit and vitamins," Nana said.

"And they taste good, too," Avry agreed.

"Everything tastes better when you are with people you love," Atreus said.

The road took them through the mountains. There were towering rock walls, little waterfalls, and running streams.

Dr. Kimberly Brayman

"Look!" Atreus shouted. "Those bighorn sheep are playing soccer."

"My friends are there," Marshmallow said. He pointed to the two large, black bears playing goalie. Nana stopped the car for a while so they could all watch.

Avry cheered when the sheep scored a goal. "I think they won the game."

There were beavers sitting on the rocks shouting loudly. "Hurrah, hurray," they said as they slapped their tails. "The Bighorn Bruisers won."

"What fun, what fun," Marshmallow said. He tried to slap his tail like the beavers, but it only made a whoosh sound.

Chapter 7: Tunnels

Avry saw a large, dark tunnel in the mountain. They were about to go through it. Her belly tightened up. Atreus watched as her face grew pale. Marshmallow saw her body tense. In a flash, Anxiety was sitting on Avry's lap.

Nana watched her in the rear-view mirror. She sang a funny song.

"She's a fairy, not a troll.

Avry can get through this hole.

Past the rocks, into the light,

We will find our friendship bright.

Through the tunnels we will go,

Holding hands and breathing slow."

As they went through the first tunnel, Avry could hear Anxiety shouting.

"I'm scaring you. I'm scaring you," Anxiety said gleefully.

Atreus smiled at Avry and held her hand. He pointed to inside the tunnel. "Look Avry!" There were fairies lighting the tunnel for them. "This is an adventure. We can do this." Atreus squeezed Avry's hand.

Marshmallow said, "Look past the darkness and you will see light, Avry."

Nana kept singing.

"She's a fairy, not a troll.

Avry can get through this hole.

Past the rocks, into the light,

We will find our friendship bright.

Through the tunnels we will go,

Holding hands and breathing slow."

Avry sighed with relief as they came out the other side. Then there was another tunnel. Avry took a slow breath. She watched the fairies light the way. Out the other side they came. "That was a little easier," Avry said.

"Here's another tunnel, Avry. It's getting easier isn't it?" Marshmallow said.

"A little," Avry said. Her tummy was still a bit wobbly.

By the sixth tunnel, Avry only had a tiny tickle left in her tummy. "I feel okay," she told Marshmallow, Nana, and Atreus. "I'm mostly not afraid of the tunnels."

"Hurray," sang Atreus. "You are so brave."

Chapter 8: Skipping Stones

After the tunnels they could see the river as it followed along the highway. Nana slowed and drove into a pullout on the side of the road. The four of them ran down to the edge of the river.

"Let's skip stones," Nana said. She showed them how to hold the flat rocks and how to throw them.

At first when Avry and Atreus threw them, the stones sank. Then Avry shouted, "I got it to skip once."

Atreus tried again. "Look, mine skipped twice."

Marshmallow looked at them both. "I can make a stone skip five times," he bragged. He held the stone just right and it skipped across the water, five times. He was grinning from ear to crooked ear.

Atreus said, "Avry, remember how we learned to skate last winter? If we keep practicing skipping stones we'll get better."

Nana threw twenty stones at once and they all sank. Everyone laughed. "My rocks were too heavy," she said, "but it was fun to try."

Chapter 9: The Hot Springs

"We're here!" Avry rolled down the window. "We are so far up in the mountains, it's snowing!"

"It's always colder in the mountains," Nana said.

Avry laughed. "Oh, look over there! Those elves are having a steam bath."

"This is the biggest swimming pool I've ever seen," Atreus said, "and I love to swim everywhere we go."

Marshmallow looked at the water and thought there was no way he was going into the hot springs. Avry knew he didn't like water, but she had a solution for him.

Once they were in their room, everyone found a place to put their things. Avry looked around and took long, deep, soft breaths. All the tension in her body slowly disappeared. Avry wasn't ready to go in the water just yet. She and Atreus played frisbee, and then did handstands.

Nana watched them play as she floated. She loved the water.

Marshmallow meowed loudly. "Look Avry! The steam coming off the pool is full of magic dust."

Avry laughed as she watched the dust settle on his bright orange fur.

"This is wonderful," Nana said. "Come one in!"

Avry and Atreus put on their bathing suits and went into the hot springs with Nana. Marshmallow joined them.

By late afternoon they'd had enough and got out.

"Let's keep adventuring," Nana suggested. "I think there's an old ghost town around here somewhere."

"Cool," Atreus said.

Avry agreed, but Marshmallow wasn't sure. He did not want to get dirty after his steam bath.

They had not gone far when Nana pulled off to the side of the road. "Well, this isn't where I thought we should be," she said. "We aren't really lost. Maybe I just took the wrong road, in the wrong state, going the wrong way." She giggled.

Avry's belly tightened. "Lost? Nana! Why are you laughing?"

Nana winked. "I love an adventure."

Atreus leaned forward. "Nana, let's use the GPS."

"Here's my big road atlas, Atreus." Nana reached down and pulled out a big book. "We can use this instead."

The atlas was dogeared and wrinkled, and Nana had clearly spilled coffee on it many times. "This is awesome," Atreus said. "We can all look at the map. Sometimes life takes us where we aren't expecting!"

Marshmallow pulled out the list he had written at Dr.

Kimberly's office. "*When things don't go as planned, have a growth mindset.* What does that mean?" he asked Atreus. "I should have paid more attention."

"It means we are going to figure this out, silly cat," Atreus said. "Woohoo! I love figuring things out."

Marshmallow looked grumpy, thinking of the pizza he wanted to be eating right about now.

"Being mad or grumpy won't help us, Marshmallow," Avry said. "We can problem solve." They all looked at the map.

"I think we are here," Atreus said. "See how the road bends ahead, and then there's another road going off that way?

"I think you are right." Nana pointed to a squiggly line. "We will guess and go this way," she said, and off they went again.

Chapter 10: Pizza Time!

Nana drove for a few minutes and before they knew it, they were in a small town. "Why are we here?" Marshmallow asked.

"One of my favorite restaurants is here," Nana said. She pulled into a parking lot and stopped the car.

Marshmallow looked up at the sign. ""Pizza!" he said. "I'm hungry."

"We all are," Avry said, as they went inside and settled in the booth.

Nana ordered pizza and drinks. When it came they all watched Marshmallow eat pizza until his already big belly overflowed and spilled out of the chair.

"This is delicious," Atreus said. He almost loved pizza as much as Marshmallow did.

"Extraordinary," Marshmallow agreed, ignoring the pizza sauce on his face.

"It's a perfect meal with friends I love," Avry said. "Can this be a celebration, Nana?"

Nana smiled. "What a good idea, Avry. We should celebrate." She called over a server, and in a few moments they all had colorful party hats.

A curious fairy, who had been sprinkling fairy dust on the pizza, asked, "What are we celebrating?"

"All of us relaxed at the hot springs," Marshmallow told her.

"Anxiety got way, way smaller," Avry added.

"And," Atreus said, "Avry isn't afraid of tunnels anymore."

Avery took another slice of pizza. "Maybe a tiny bit still, but we will practice more on our trip home."

"That is exactly what we will do," Nana said.

Atreus smiled. "Maybe there will be another bighorn sheep soccer game we can see tomorrow."

"I'm cheering with the beavers," Marshmallow said. "They do have better tails than I do, though. I'll just cheer louder."

"Oh, Marshmallow," Avry said, feeling a little bit wise. "Remember that we need to do our best, and that is all anyone can ask of us."

Strategies For Anxiety

1. Extra weight such as a pet or weighted blanket can decrease a child's anxiety.

2. Research solidly supports having an animal as emotional support. In some countries, a psychologist or mental health professional can assess a child's needs, and an animal's suitability for this designation. There are special rights for these animals when they are part of a child's treatment plan.

3. Telling someone they shouldn't feel what they do, doesn't help. Helping them access new skills, will. A psychologist/therapist can help them learn coping skills and strategies. Please ask the professional what their specific training with children is.

4. It's helpful to know what anxiety symptoms your child has so you and they can understand what is happening, and can name it: " I feel anxious." Just saying that helps a tiny bit. List the anxiety symptoms that your loved little one has. Ask them to help.

5. Soft-belly breathing that allows the diaphragm to lower (and breathing to slow) helps decrease anxiety.

6. Learning to be self-reflective and challenge irrational thoughts is a Mega Skill: it helps with living life better. It's a huge part of dealing effectively with anxiety. Making wise choices regarding the level of stimulation and the length of high stimulation (noisy crowds) assists in feelings of control. Some simple things to help include:
    *   sitting at the edge of a restaurant in a booth vs sitting at a table in the middle surrounded by people
    *   negotiating how long to stay at high-intensity events

- learning how to quietly regroup
- scheduling in quiet time as an essential part of each day
- learning to self-identify where one is on the "calm-to-overwhelmed" scale, and intervene before meltdown.

All these are part of skill building.

7.   Behavioral choices (such as relaxation breathing, decreasing stimulation, grounding into the earth), and "thinking" choices (such as challenging irrational thoughts) will decrease anxiety. Unfortunately, anxiety often gets worse close to adolescence as hormones kick in. The good news is the potential for working with it also improves with abstract thought.

8.   Children who are creative (and anxious) need to be encouraged to focus on what they are good at, and get extra support or tutoring at what they struggle with.

9.   Having skills or abilities boosts self-esteem. Feeling capable and worthwhile also encourages making better decisions. Help a struggling child learn to do something. Indirectly this benefits mood and decreases anxiety.

10.   All children need a support network that they can access for help. If you have anxiety it's doubly important. Self-reliance needs to be encouraged and yet we all need to feel like we belong and have people to love us.

11.   Connection with others lowers the stress hormone and can soften anxiety. Distraction can sometimes help, like a funny song.

12. "Desensitization" is being exposed to something repeatedly until the anxiety response decreases. Avry does this by going through multiple tunnels. Desensitization should only be done under the skilled supervision of a psychologist.

13. Children and adults benefit from time in nature and/or time taking warm (or sometimes cold) showers or baths. Here, the hots springs are very relaxing. This can be one coping skill they will know how to use.

14. How we "frame" a situation makes a world of difference. Is it a catastrophe or an adventure? Is it a defeat, a mistake, or is it a challenge to be overcome? Remember that our children learn by watching and listening to us.

NOTE: This book is not intended to replace assessment and treatment with a therapist or psychologist who specializes in work with children. It was written as a magical story with some helpful ideas.

About the Author

Dr. Kimberly Brayman is a psychologist who resides in British Columbia, Canada.

After decades of working in health care, she is inspired to build confidence, normalize struggle, encourage hope, and delight adults and children alike through her storytelling.

She believes stories build empathy and empower the listener to find their own self-reliance and strength.

The power of supportive relationships is a theme that runs through all her books.

When a child knows deep in their heart that they are loved and accepted, just the way they are, they have a chance to blossom and thrive.

In this series, Avry is a highly sensitive, anxious girl who develops capability and courage and gains insight with every adventure.

Her magic cat, Marshmallow, is her best friend and near-constant companion. They are joined by friends, family members, elves, fairies, animals, and magic in this series.

Dr. Kimberly Brayman is a registered psychologist (registration #2464) in British Columbia, Canada.

About the Illustrator

Irina Denissova loves creating illustrations for children's books. Her creative talents bring a magical atmosphere to stories, making them enjoyable for both parents and children. She believes the best part about being an illustrator is that she helps create a new world for readers.

She lives in Temirtau, Kazakhstan and, in her spare time, loves to read and create whatever drawings pop into her mind.

The author describes her as a humble, unbelievably talented young woman who has a near-magical ability to take descriptions and characters and create what the author sees in her own mind.

Other Marshmallow the Magic Cat Adventures, available on Amazon

Avry's Magical Cat
Avry adopts a magical cat from the animal shelter. Avry has a magical view of the world, and every day she learns the value of good friends, love and family.

A Troll in the Woods
A true quest that shows courage and fear can go hand in hand, and the power of friendship can inspire action.

Avry and Atreus Save Christmas
A delightful Christmas tale to be read every holiday season. It's full of elves, ravens and the capability inside all children to redeem themselves and be good.

Marshmallow Paints the Town
A fun story that focuses on collaboration, self-responsibility, making mistakes, and recovering.

Marshmallow Gets a Little Sister
Avry brings home a stray kitten, which makes Marshmallow very unhappy. He does not want a little sister and he wants to get rid of her. Is there really enough love to go around?

Visit the author's website at KimberlyBraymanAuthor.com for updates.

Get all the Marshmallow
books at Amazon today!

Other Illustrated Children's Books by Dr. Kimberly Brayman on Amazon

Artsy Alphabet

Nana Loves You More

I Want to Be

Will You Be My Friend?

Count With Me!

Blueberries

We Are Different and the Same

The Magical Fisherman

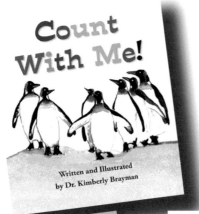

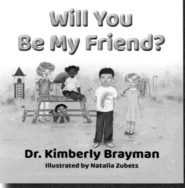

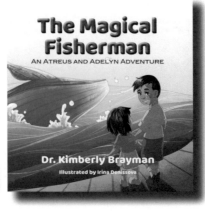

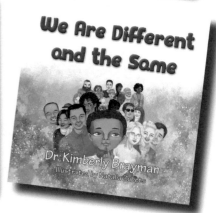

Check out the new Sibley books on Amazon.

Made in United States
Troutdale, OR
01/27/2024